# Apple Crumble

Mum had just left a hot apple crumble on the kitchen table. Pip and Tess smelt the apple crumble. "That was my tum grumbling and rumbling," said Pip.

"Let's have a nibble from that crumble,"
said Tess. "I will guzzle it up!" said Pip.
So the little ants crept up to the dish.
"It is too hot!" grumbled Pip. "Then
just nibble a little bit," said Tess.

But the apple crumble was still too
hot. "Let's dig into the crumble," said
Pip. "We can tip it onto the table."
So the little ants dug into the
crumble and tipped it on the table.

Nibble, nibble, went Tess. Guzzle, guzzle, went Pip. Pip got back onto the dish. He began to wobble. He wobbled and tumbled into the dish. He struggled to get off the crumble.

Just then, the little ant was swept up and tipped onto a little dish. "Oh no!" thinks Tess, "Pip will be gobbled up by that kid. Stop!" Pip was frantic.

"I will not be gobbled up!" Pip yelled.

Pip kicked and scrambled to get off.

"Help!" Just then, the kid picked up

the little ant and let him go.

"Little ant, I am not fond of apple

crumble with ants on top!" said the kid.

# Reading practice and lotto game

Use this page as a two-syllable reading exercise.
You can also photocopy this page and use it to play as a lotto game.
Enlarge and photocopy the set of cards twice on different
coloured card. Cut up one set to make the cards. Cut the other
page in half to make two bases.

| jum/ble jumble | han/dle handle | sim/ple simple |
|---|---|---|
| grum/ble grumble | jun/gle jungle | bu/ckle buckle |

| mum/ble mumble | can/dle candle | crum/ple crumple |
|---|---|---|
| crum/ble crumble | jin/gle jingle | ti/ckle tickle |